You're Safe Now, Waterdog

Richard Edwards

Illustrated by
Sophy Williams

Orion
Children's Books

First published in Great Britain in 1996
by Orion Children's Books
a division of the Orion Publishing Group Ltd
Orion House
5 Upper St Martin's Lane
London WC2H 9EA

A catalogue record for this book is available from the British Library
Printed in Italy
Designed by Dalia Hartman

ISBN 1 85881 279 8

Watt the dog and Matt were always together.

They played together.

They went shopping together.

They curled up in the same bed together.

Matt took Watt everywhere…

…exploring,

climbing,

even to school.

But as Matt grew up he began to forget about Watt the dog.

So sometimes Watt stayed at home when Matt went out on his bicycle, or sat cramped in a dusty corner when Matt got into bed.

One day after Matt had been out
playing with his friends, Watt was left
behind on the river bank, and no one
came back to look for him.

Watt lay all alone beside the river.
Owls hooted in the treetops, and
a fox sniffed at Watt before slinking
away into the darkness.

Then it began to rain.

Rain fell on the woods and fields. Rain
filled the ditches and poured into the river
until the water swirled round Watt, lifting
him up and carrying him away.

Spinning and ducking, Watt the waterdog drifted downstream, past herds of staring cows, past farms and fishermen, through villages, under bridges.

At first he floated well, but the longer his journey
lasted the colder and soggier he got, until only his head
was left bobbing above the surface.

Hattie was splashing about
by the river trying to scoop up
leaves when Watt drifted past.

She reached out with her net but missed. She reached again and missed again, but the third time she stretched just far enough to lift Watt out of the water and carry him proudly home.

"Look. A waterdog!"

Watt lay in front of a warm fire, gently steaming. When he was dry he sat at the table while Hattie ate her supper.

At bedtime Hattie carried Watt to her room and tucked him into a shoebox on her bedside table.

But when the light was out and the door was closed, she lifted him out of the box.

"You're safe now, waterdog," she whispered.

And she hugged him tight and fell asleep with Watt the Waterdog cuddled in her arms.